Discard

CELEBRATIONS

MYRA COHN LIVINGSTON
POET

LEONARD EVERETT FISHER
PAINTER

Holiday House   New York

This book was set in Palatino type by American-Stratford
Graphic Services, Inc.
Color separations were made by Capper, Inc.
It was printed on Moistrite Matte by Rae Publishing Co.
and bound by Bookbinders, Inc.
Typography by David Rogers

The art was prepared with acrylic paint, the same size as it
appears in the book. The pictures were created on a
textured paper and then peeled from the back of the paper
in preparation for laser light scanning.

Library of Congress Cataloging in Publication Data

Livingston, Myra Cohn.
  Celebrations.

  SUMMARY: A collection of poems on the holidays of the
year, from New Year's Day through Martin Luther King
Day, Passover, Labor Day, Halloween, and others, to
Christmas Eve.
  1. Holidays—Juvenile poetry. 2. Children's poetry,
American. [1. Holidays—Poetry] I. Fisher, Leonard
Everett, ill. II. Title.
PS3562.I945C4 1985   811'.54   84-19216
ISBN 0-8234-0550-8
ISBN 0-8234-0654-7 (pbk.)

CONTENTS

NEW YEAR'S EVE

Play a thin tune
on a paper horn.
    Old is dying.
    New is born.

Scatter confetti
over the floor.
    Sweep an old year
    Out the door.

Blow up a wish
in a bright balloon.
    Whisper dreams
    To a midnight moon.

Play a loud tune
on a paper horn.
    Old is dying.
    New is born.

MARTIN LUTHER KING DAY

The dream
of Martin Luther King
will happen
in some far-off Spring

when winter ice
and snow are gone.
One day, the dreamer
in gray dawn

will waken
to a blinding light
where hawk and dove
in silent flight

brush wings together
on a street
still thundering
with ghostly feet.

And soul will dance
and soul will sing
and march with
Martin Luther King.

PRESIDENTS' DAY

Remembering
what came before,
we raise old flags
in peace, in war.

Remembering
their names, their birth—
we fuse stone monuments
to earth.

Remembering
the brave, the great,
we mark these days
to celebrate.

Remembering
that we are free—
we write their lives
in history.

MY VALENTINE

My Valentine
Has eyes of green
With twenty eyebrows in between.
Her skin is blue.
Her head is square.
She hasn't got a brain in there.
Her four ears twitch.
Her noses shine
But still,
(I think,)
I'll make her mine!

SAINT PATRICK'S DAY

Green
is in my head;
green for an island
evergreen with wood sorrel
creeping over a great stone chair;
pipers dancing on green turf;
green snakes drowning in the sea;

There, Saint Patrick stands
holding a shamrock

and I take it
for Ireland—
and wear its green.

APRIL FOOL

The maple syrup's full of ants.
                    A mouse is creeping on the shelf.

                    Is that a spider on your back?
I ate the whole pie by myself.

The kitchen sink just overflowed.
                    A flash flood washed away the school.
I threw your blanket in the trash.

                    I never lie———I———
                              APRIL FOOL!

PASSOVER

Out of a land
that held us slaves,

Under the wings
of the angel of death,

Over hot sands,
across cold seas,

We sing again
with freedom's breath.

EASTER: FOR PENNY

At Easter wild grass is left to grow
for hiding eggs in nests of scraggly green,
and Mama has a way to let us know

where we can run, and where to walk real slow
along the slippery edge of the ravine.
At Easter wild grass is left to grow

so we can search the darkest spots to go
where shining pennies sparkle in between
and Mama has a way to let us know

how blades pull back, and how to look real low
for colored eggs and tiny jelly beans.
At Easter wild grass is left to grow.

We break the shells with bare feet, stub a toe
where clay has hardened into clots unseen,
and Mama has a way to let us know

to count on what is hidden down below,
no matter times be good or times be lean.
At Easter wild grass is left to grow
and Mama has a way to let us know . . .

MEMORIAL DAY

This,
the flag
that marks a grave.

This,
the bugle
blasting the sky.

This,
the poppy
red as blood.

This,
the parade
for the last to die.

FOURTH OF JULY

Hurrah for the Fourth of July
When fireworks burst in the sky!
All you need is a match
And a quick little scratch
And a rocket and fuse and——GOOD-BYE

20

LABOR DAY

Packing
up her picnic,
pouring cold lemonade
in the park grass, Summer says
good-bye!

COLUMBUS DAY

Across the world,
Columbus,
you dreamt your wild schemes.

You slept on decks
of sailing ships;
you nailed the wooden beams.

You coaxed west wind
into the sails;
you mended tattered seams.

Across the world,
Columbus,
you brought your wild dreams.

HALLOWEEN

Green cat eyes
in midnight gloom
fly with the witch
on her ragged broom
over dark hills
where bonfires loom.

There, where haunted
spirits groan,
crouched in the rubble
of rag and bone,
Old Halloween
unearths gray stone

counting the souls
of the restless dead,
nodding her wizened,
shrouded head.
Then, with her bony
fingers spread

she bids them dance
to a frenzied tune.
Thin bodies floating
circle the moon,
and Old Halloween
falls in a swoon . . .

Red embers die
as the hillside shakes.
A rooster crows.
The morning breaks.
The witch lies dead.
The cat awakes.

THANKSGIVING

Pilgrims
move among us.
Silent, their gray lips mouth
prayers for the bountiful fields of
autumn.

Feathered
Indians stand
tall in quiet corners
invoking harvest home in a
strange tongue.

This is
our Thanksgiving.
Gathered together, we
are visited by the grace of
old guests.

CHRISTMAS EVE

He is coming,
I know,
Through the dark sky,
Through snow.
On this cold winter night
Quietly,
Out of sight,
He is coming from far
By the light of a star.

He remembers,
I know,
All the gifts
Long ago.
Gifts that promise delight
When the dark turns to light.
He has listened and heard
Every wish, every word.

He has come
And is gone
When we wake
In the dawn.
When we gather around
He will know what is found.
He will come,
I believe.
He will come
Christmas Eve.

BIRTHDAY

When he asked for the moon
they laughed
and said
that his birthday wish
was wrong

and the little boy cried
and went
outside
and he looked at the moon
so long

that it floated to where
his eyes
looked up
and it shimmered him
in its light

and the little boy knew
as his wish
came true
that a birthday wish
is right.

LEF